This book belongs to:

_____

This paperback edition first published in 2010 by Andersen Press Ltd.
Published in Australia by Random House Australia Pty.,
Level 3, 100 Pacific Highway, North Sydney, NSW 2060.
First published in Great Britain in 1972 by Hamish Hamilton.
Text copyright © John Yeoman, 1972.
Illustration copyright © Quentin Blake, 1972
The rights of John Yeoman and Quentin Blake to be identified as the
author and illustrator of this work have been asserted by them
in accordance with the Copyright, Designs and Patents Act, 1988.
All rights reserved.
Printed in China.
Quentin Blake has used pen, ink and watercolour in this book.

10   9   8   7   6   5   4   3   2   1

British Library Cataloguing in Publication Data available.

Trade ISBN 978 1 84939 201 3

Special Sales ISBN 978 1 78344 236 2

This book has been printed on acid-free paper

John Yeoman Quentin Blake

MOUSE TROUBLE

ANDERSEN PRESS

A long, long time ago there stood an old windmill, perched on the top of a hill. In its day it had been a very fine windmill, but the miller who owned it now was a mean, bad-tempered man, who would never spend money on repairs. There was one thing that made him especially grumpy – mouse trouble.

There were hundreds of mice in the old mill
and they loved it there. They didn't mind the noise of
the creaking machinery, grinding away. They had
a marvellous time using the great millstone
as a roundabout . . .

. . . balancing on the
turning beams . . .

. . . and sliding down
the grain chutes.

They were so happy in the mill that often, on clear moonlit nights, when the sails had stopped turning and the machinery was still, they would form a circle around their leader – a white mouse who had escaped from a pet-shop – and tell mouse jokes and sing songs in their high twittery voices.

Although he never saw the mice, the grumpy miller knew they were there by their footprints, and the nibbled sacks, and the twittery singing in the dark.

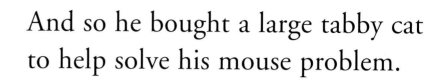

And so he bought a large tabby cat
to help solve his mouse problem.

But the miller was so mean that he wouldn't give the
cat anything to eat and used to kick him, too. As a
result the cat moped about, worrying because he knew
he wasn't fit enough to catch any of those frisky mice.

The mice, though, felt rather sorry for the tabby and were unhappy to see him looking so down in the mouth. The white mouse called a meeting. "That cat needs more exercise," he said. "We must make it easier for him to chase us."

"What good will that do?" asked a fat little piebald mouse.

"It will make him fitter and happier – and it will provide us with some good games," said the white mouse.

At this they all twittered with delight.

And so they began to make life more exciting for the cat. Sometimes they sat on the turning sails and made rude faces at him when they glided past his favourite seat at the window.

Sometimes they covered him with the flour dust that had settled on the ledges and shelves. Sometimes the younger mice let the tabby see them and chase them. And they always pretended to be terrified of him, so that he'd have something to feel proud about.

And, sure enough, it all began to have an effect on the tabby. He started to take a pride in himself. One day the white mouse sat watching him practise in front of a broken mirror in the outhouse.

First he practised slinking up to a screwdriver as though it were a mouse.

Then he practised pouncing on it ferociously.

And then he practised being thanked by the grateful miller.

The white mouse enjoyed this immensely and said aloud, in his best quivery voice, "Oh bless my soul, what a terrifying cat! I feel quite faint."
And with that he scampered off.

As the cat grew livelier, the mice became even happier.
Every night, while the cat slept soundly after his efforts
to keep the mice in order, they all came out to celebrate.
Swarms of the younger ones would scuttle up and down
the ladder staircases with squeaks of delight, while the
older ones sat in the pockets of the workmen's aprons
hanging on the wall and looked on contentedly.
They thought how much nicer the world had
become since their younger days.

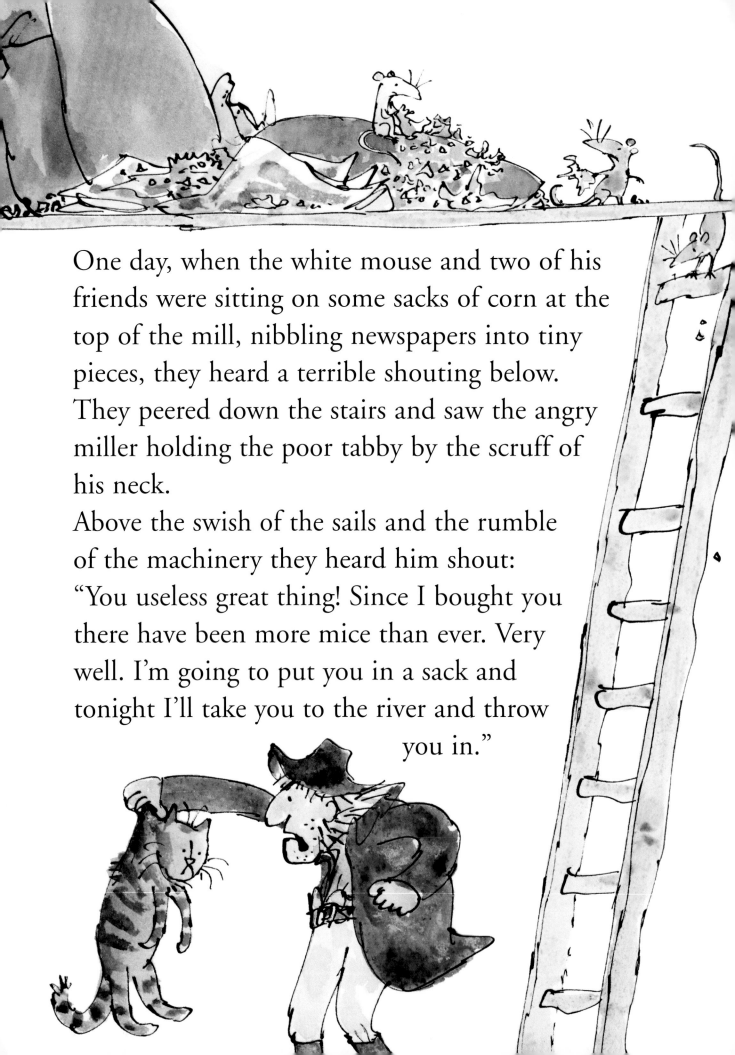

One day, when the white mouse and two of his friends were sitting on some sacks of corn at the top of the mill, nibbling newspapers into tiny pieces, they heard a terrible shouting below. They peered down the stairs and saw the angry miller holding the poor tabby by the scruff of his neck.

Above the swish of the sails and the rumble of the machinery they heard him shout: "You useless great thing! Since I bought you there have been more mice than ever. Very well. I'm going to put you in a sack and tonight I'll take you to the river and throw you in."

The mice were very upset and begged the white mouse to do something. So, as soon as it was safe, he led a crowd of them into the outhouse where the miller had taken the cat. The wretched animal was already tied up in a sack, so the white mouse climbed on to what he imagined was the cat's shoulder and whispered into what was probably the cat's ear.

"My fellow mice," he whispered, "ask me to say that although you are our dreaded enemy, we don't want you to be drowned. If we help you to escape, will you promise to be friends with us afterwards?"
The poor trembling bundle nodded its head.
"Right," said the white mouse, and he gave out instructions.

One group, led by the white mouse, crept into the hallway of the mill and quietly unhooked the miller's wife's fur cape from its peg.

Carrying it above their heads, they scampered back to
the outhouse.

When they got there, another group had already
nibbled through the string which was tied round the
sack, and the cat was free and panting with relief.

In no time some of the mice stuffed the fur cape with straw, while some particularly strong ones dragged along a horseshoe so that they could make the sack heavier.

Then they filled the sack and tied it up again. "That stupid miller will never know the difference," said the white mouse.

That night the miller took his sack down the lane to the river, followed – although he didn't know it – by hundreds of inquisitive mice.

They sat on the wall of the bridge and watched him fling the bundle into the water with a great splash. "That's the last we'll see of him," said the miller with a snort. And he set off home with the mice silently following him again.

The miller decided that cats were no use and he never bought another one. But he didn't know that the great tabby, still alive and much more contented than he'd ever been, was living with the mice on the very top floor of the mill, eating all the best titbits they could find for him in the larder . . .

. . . and playing endless games of cat and mouse.

Also by John Yeoman and Quentin Blake:

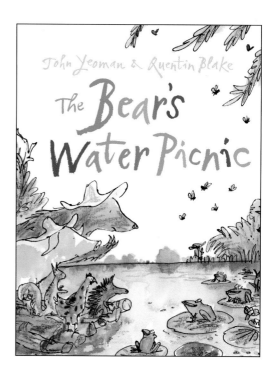